Because everyone loves a good story...

Alanna Books

To my daddy, whose stories about the preachán
and the bodach were the best, and
to Martha for changing my life, with love Anna
To Marion, and the magnificent Milroys, with love Ros

First published in paperback in the UK in 2011 by
Alanna Books
46 Chalvey Road East,
Slough, Berkshire, SL1 2LR

www.alannabooks.com

ISBN: 978-1-907825-01-9

Printed and bound in China

Lulu loves Stories

Anna McQuinn

Illustrated by Rosalind Beardshaw

ALANNA BOOKS

On Saturdays, Lulu's daddy takes her to the library.

The library is VERY busy on Saturdays,

but Lulu still finds some excellent books.

When they come home,
Lulu's daddy reads
the first story.

It's about a fabulous fairy princess!

All the next day,
Lulu is a fairy princess.

She has a magical dress
and a sparkly crown.

She's just fabulous!

On Sunday night, Lulu and her mummy read the next story. It's about an amazing journey.

All day Monday, Lulu takes her friends on fantastic trips to exotic places like Paris and Lagos.

On Tuesday, Lulu chooses a story about friends.

All afternoon, she and Ben play
cafés with their babies. Lulu has
cappuccino and her baby has juice.

Tuesday night, Lulu's mummy
reads a story about fierce tigers!

Next day, Lulu chases her friend
Orla all over the jungle.

Wednesday night, Lulu reads a story
about Old MacDonald's farm
and all next day, she is a farmer.
Taking care of the animals
is tough work!

Lulu's cow is sick!

Luckily mummy knows
how to make her better.

Thursday night, Lulu and her daddy read about building.

Next day, Lulu has to fix up her house.
She needs a hammer, a saw...
and a little help from daddy.

Friday night, Lulu's daddy makes up
a story about a little girl who
has a magic pair of shoes.
Next day, Lulu's shoes
are truly magical.

They sparkle all the way
to the library...

...and all the way home.

They even sparkle while her daddy reads her a story about a wild and wicked monster!

What will Lulu be tomorrow?

Alanna Books is a small independent publisher.

We aim to produce books that celebrate children -
With so much pressure to conform,
life can be difficult for those who seem different
or who choose to be individual.
Alanna celebrates what makes each of us unique
while also believing that,
deep down, we are far more alike than we are different...

and that **everyone** loves a good story!

More from **Alanna Books**
the best in home-grown picture books...

If you have only just met Lulu, you must also seek out
Lulu Loves the Library.
It's also available in paperback with a free CD
and as a boardbook – with shorter simpler text – perfect for toddlers.
Lulu Loves Stories is also available as a shorter boardbook.
And look our for Lulu's newest adventure – she's going to have a new baby
brother to share her stories with!

978-0-9551998-20

978-0-9551998-75

978-1-907825-002

and the best from around the world...

In **Splendid Friend, Indeed**, meet shy Bear and vivacious Goose.
"Picture book perfection!"
Alanna is delighted to make this multi-award winning title
from the USA available for the first time in the UK.

978-0-9551998-99

In **Little Frog**, meet VERY naughty Frog.
He thinks his parents don't love him
any more and has to go on a long journey
to discover that they do.
Another multi-award winning title
from one of Denmark's premier cartoonists
brought to the UK by Alanna Books.

978-0-9551998-68

www.alannabooks.com

Anna McQuinn works part time as a community librarian, working with a diverse group of children and parents. Many of the children speak different languages at home which can make storytime challenging, so Anna recorded the parents telling **Lulu Loves Stories** in their first language. This one CD contains a selection of langauges and Alanna Books hopes you enjoy it whichever one you speak!

- If you and your child speak English as a first language you can listen to the story in English. It is also fascinating to listen to a little of the story in other languages;

- If you speak one of the languages, listen as you and your child look at the pictures together;

- If you work in any setting where children speak different home languages, play one track to a small group or use it one-to-one with a child. You can even have different languages playing in the background while you do other non-verbal activities like drawing or jigsaws.

- If you work in a library, or your group lends books to parents, with so many languages on the one CD this is a great resource. At this young age, children can't read – so dual language books are not such an effective means of validating their home language. In addition, some parents speak but do not read their first language. So listening to the story and looking at the pictures is much more fun – Enjoy!

Alanna Books makes new recordings all the time, so check the website to hear more langauges.